THE HEIGHTS

River

SADDLEBACK
EDUCATIONAL PUBLISHING

Original text by Ed Hansen
Adapted by Mary Kate Doman

SADDLEBACK
EDUCATIONAL PUBLISHING
www.sdlback.com

Copyright © 2011 by Saddleback Educational Publishing

ISBN-13: 978-1-61651-281-1
ISBN-10: 1-61651-281-4
eBook: 978-1-60291-682-1

Printed in Guangzhou, China
1110/11-01-10

16 15 14 13 12   1 2 3 4 5

Chapter 1

The small airport was quiet. It was in western Brazil. Rafael Silva was waiting.

A plane landed. Rafael saw his kids. He ran toward them.

"You guys look great!" he said. "I can't wait to show you around."

Franco, the oldest at 16, laughed. "We're excited, Dad."

"I missed you," eleven-year-old Lilia said.

Antonio, 13, gave his dad a fist bump. "The flight rocked!"

They got their bags. Then they got a taxi. It was old. And its engine popped.

"Where *are* we, Dad?" Franco asked. "We're going to your job. Right? Where is the dam?"

"That's right," Rafael said. "That airport is closed. So we'll take a boat."

"Cool! A boat! Up the Amazon River!" Lilia sang out.

They crossed a busy street. A soccer ball bounced ahead. The taxi stopped fast. The driver yelled.

They drove out of town. The street was bumpy. There were lots of green trees.

"Here we are," Rafael said. "There's the dock."

"Yuck! That river looks dirty," Lilia cried.

The brown water was moving fast. It was hard to see the other side.

"I didn't think the river would be this wide!" said Franco.

"It's one of the world's largest rivers. Some places it's a lot wider," Rafael said.

Rafael paid the taxi driver. They got their bags.

"There's only one boat," Franco said. "So I guess it must be ours."

"That's it," said Rafael. "That's the *Amazon Queen*."

"It's falling apart," Antonio said.

The old boat needed fixing. Its paint was cracked. There was rust.

"Is it safe?" Antonio asked.

Rafael nodded. "This boat is over 30 years old. Never been in an accident. Or so says Captain Dias."

Just then a man appeared.

"Silva?" he called out.

"Yes, I'm Rafael Silva."

The man had red eyes. His hair was messy. His clothes were dirty.

The man frowned.

"I am Captain Renato," he said.

Rafael looked confused.

"But where is Captain Dias?" he asked.

"Sick. Got fever. No problem. I take you."

Chapter 2

The Silvas stood on the *Amazon Queen*. The view was great. The trees looked huge. The trunks leaned out over the river. Colorful birds flew around.

Rafael grew up in Brazil. He moved to the U.S. And he decided to stay. But his Portuguese was still good. He wanted to speak to the captain.

Rafael looked into the control room. Inside, Captain Renato was steering the boat. He had a brown bottle. Rafael watched. The captain took a drink from it. Rafael thought it was alcohol.

He thought Captain Renato was okay. "So far, so good," he said to himself. "But I'll keep my eyes open." He returned to the kids.

"Dad," Lilia asked, "what are those?"

She pointed to some dark shapes.

"They look like logs. But they keep moving," Lilia said.

"They're caimans," Rafael said. "Like alligators."

Lilia gulped. "Are they as dangerous?" she asked in a small voice.

The caimans moved. They headed toward the boat.

One of the caimans opened its mouth. Lilia squeezed closer to her father.

Antonio gasped.

And Franco said, "Wow, look at that! Those teeth are huge!"

"They think we may have food," Rafael said.

"Food?" asked Franco. "You mean *us*?"

The Melo family joined them. They were heading for home. They lived in a river village. It would take time to get there. The two families were the only passengers.

The river got wider. Then the sun began to set.

Now Captain Renato was turning the boat. They were going toward shore.

"Are we stopping?" Lilia asked.

"It's not safe on the river at night," Rafael said. "There are no lights. And lots of animals come out."

Lilia looked scared. Her father patted her shoulder.

"We'll be all right. Don't worry. We'll sleep on the boat. It will be safe at the dock."

It didn't take long. The boat pulled up to a dock. The dock was made from wood.

Dinner was next. Then they went to their bunks. The Silvas were in one cabin. It was small. The jungle was noisy. The night air was calm.

And the Silvas could hear a lot.

There was a loud roar. And then another. There were hisses. And squeaks. And long howls.

The strange noises went on. But the tired Silvas finally went to sleep.

Chapter 3

Nobody slept well. The jungle was too loud. The sun rose. But they were all awake.

The boat began to shake. The engine started. Minutes later, the *Amazon Queen* was moving.

Rafael frowned. He saw the captain drinking.

It was late morning. The boat moved to shore. It moved slowly to a dock.

"Look over there. It's a village!" Antonio shouted.

"Hey, I bet that's the Melo's village," Lilia cried.

Many villagers came out. They greeted the Melo family home. They smiled and waved. The Melos got off.

Then the boat pulled away. The Melos waved goodbye. The Silvas waved back.

It was afternoon. And the sun was hot. The boat was far from the village. The Silvas were too tired to do anything. They sat.

There was a loud splash. It was on the other side of the boat.

"Did you hear that?" Lilia asked.

Rafael got up. He went around the control room to look.

"I can't see anything," he said.

Then Antonio shouted, *"The captain! Where is he?"*

Rafael ran to the back of the boat. He looked in the river. Everyone joined him.

An arm reached out of the water. It was the captain! Big, dark shapes were swimming toward him.

"Caimans!" Franco cried.

In seconds, the caimans seemed to be fighting. Then the water was red.

The Silvas stared. They were upset.

Rafael ran into the control room. He searched for the control. He wanted to drive the boat.

Then the engine died. He worked with the control. But for some reason the engine wouldn't start.

"Look!" Antonio shouted. He pointed up ahead.

"We're going into the left fork," Rafael gasped. "We're supposed to go *right*!"

Rafael worked to turn the wheel. Franco hurried to help. Together, they tried to pull the wheel to the right. But there wasn't enough time!

The boat went left. It went down the left fork! Again, Rafael tried to start the engine. But it still wouldn't start.

"We're out of gas, Dad!" Antonio said.

Rafael was scared by Antonio's words.

"Where will this left fork take us, Dad?" Antonio asked.

Rafael gulped. "It leads into the deep jungle."

Chapter 4

Antonio stared at his father.

"What are we going to do?" he asked in a small voice.

Franco and Lilia stood beside him. All three looked scared.

"Is there anyplace we can get some gas?" Lilia wanted to know.

Rafael shook his head.

"Not here. This fork leads deep into the jungle. There won't be anywhere to get gas," he said.

"So, what can we do? We have no gas. And we're on the wrong river," said Franco.

"Stay calm, kids," Rafael said. "We'll ditch the boat. We'll go to the shore. Then we'll hike back to the Melo's village. We should be able to make it in two days. Three at the most."

"But, Dad! That means we'll be in the jungle at night," Lilia said. She was afraid.

"Don't worry. We'll find a safe place. And one of us will guard," said Rafael.

Slowly, the *Amazon Queen* crossed the wide river.

Franco was standing just outside the control room. "Dad, we're going faster!" he yelled.

Antonio shouted, "Franco's right, Dad! Our speed is *really* picking up!"

"Look!" Franco pointed at white water. "We must be heading for a waterfall!"

"Antonio and Lilia, come inside!" Rafael shouted. "I'm going to hit the shore!"

Next, everyone got in the control room.

They were very close to the shore. Franco pointed. There was a patch of ground. He called out, "There!"

Rafael turned the wheel. He turned it as far as it would go. He shouted, "Hang on tight!"

The *Amazon Queen* tilted. It hit the shore with a thud.

Franco rushed off the boat. He ran to a nearby tree. He tied a heavy rope around it. The rope held the boat in place.

"Now let's pack what we can carry. Just take key things—food, water, clothes, knives, rope. No junk," Rafael said.

Later, the shore was covered. There were a lot of things. Rafael chose only the most needed items. Then they loaded them into bags.

"Okay," Rafael said. "Let's get a fire going. We need to eat. And get some sleep. Then we'll be ready. We need to start early."

It was night. The Silvas heard a terrible sound. The water carried the boat away! It made a lot of noise.

They blinked. And they stared into the darkness. The *Amazon Queen* disappeared.

Chapter 5

They ate breakfast. Rafael reminded
the kids. Everyone needed to stay
close. No one could get lost.

"The jungle will be very thick,"
he said. "It would be easy to get lost.
But the hike shouldn't be too bad.
All we have to do is follow the river.
That way, we can't miss the village."

"Right," said Franco.

"But we don't want to get *too*

close to the shore. There are caimans. And there are piranhas in some parts of the river."

"What are *piranhas*?" Lilia asked.

"They're small fish. They have sharp teeth. And they swim in groups. They're very mean. And they can skin large animal fast," Rafael said.

It was 7 a.m. The Silvas headed into the jungle. Rafael led the way. He used a big knife to make a trail.

It was very slow. The village was far away.

They rested. Then Rafael said, "Time to go, guys. Let's get moving."

It was hot and muggy. They were all soaked with sweat. And biting bugs were everywhere. They flew in their ears and mouths!

"Go away! Go away!" Lilia shouted. She swatted at the bugs.

Rafael patted her back.

"There's a small, white flower. It will keep the bugs away," he said. "You crush the petals. Then rub them on your skin. Let's look for some, Lilia."

Minutes later, Lilia yelled. "Is this the white flower, Dad?" she asked.

Lilia had found the right plant. They crushed the petals. And rubbed them on their skin. The bugs quickly flew off.

The thick jungle suddenly opened. There was a space. Rafael stepped forward. But then he started to sink! The ground was too soft!

He knew what happened. He

found a mud pit! It was dragging him under. He was covered in mud.

Rafael warned the kids to stay back. He tried to free himself. But he couldn't. The mud was above his knees. And he was slowly being pulled deeper.

Lilia screamed at her brothers. *"Dad's sinking into the ground!"* she cried.

Chapter 6

Franco searched his bag for a piece
of rope. He was scared. He needed
that rope.

"Where did we put the rope?" he
cried. "Antonio, look in your bag."

Antonio pulled rope from his bag.
It was 25 feet. He handed it to his
brother. Franco tossed one end to
his father. Rafael was now up to his
waist in mud.

The three kids pulled on the rope. They pulled hard. But they couldn't free Rafael. The mud was thick. The suction was too strong. But at least he wasn't sinking any deeper.

Rafael realized that he'd have to free himself. He leaned back. And he used all his strength to lift his legs up.

Finally, Rafael was on top of the mud. He was floating. Inch by inch, the kids pulled their father to safety. Rafael was tired.

"That was a close one!" Antonio said.

"I'll have to be more careful," Rafael said. "Now let's get around this pit."

Soon, they came to another small

opening in the jungle. From there they could see the Amazon.

It was almost 4 o'clock. Everyone was tired. Everyone was hungry. But Rafael wanted to keep going. They'd wasted a lot of time. And he wanted to make it up.

They went on. And they made sure that they could see the river. Two hours passed. Then they found another small space.

"This looks like a good place to spend the night," Rafael said. "Let's get some firewood."

"What are our chances? Can we make it back tomorrow? To the village, I mean," Franco asked hopefully.

"We lost too much time today,"

said Rafael.

Lilia looked scared. "We don't have very much food," she said.

"We should be fine. There's lots to eat in the jungle. We just have to find it."

Chapter 7

It was a noisy night. The Silvas
heard many grunts. And shrieks.
And sharp cries. They heard parrots.
And toads. And frogs.

Antonio and Rafael took their
turns on guard. The noises slowly
stopped. It was getting light.

They found some wild fruit for
breakfast. It tasted sour. But it was
juicy and filling. They put out the

fire. Then everyone headed into the jungle.

They came to another opening. Rafael could see the Amazon River to his left. He could also see a smaller river. The Silvas stood on the shore. They studied the problem.

"Hmm, I'm guessing. This water goes into the Amazon," Franco said.

"I think you're right, Franco. But we still have to cross it. We can't go around. It might take us miles into the jungle," Rafael said.

"I think we can cross it," Lilia said. "It doesn't look that wide."

"That's not what I'm worried about," said Rafael. "We don't know how *deep* it is. Or what animals might be living in it."

"Oh, right! I forgot about caimans and piranhas!" Lilia cried.

Antonio saw a tree trunk. It was on the ground. "Look, Dad!" he said. "Maybe we can use that to float across."

"Yeah," Franco agreed. "We can cut some branches. Then we can pole across. We won't even get wet."

"It might work. It just might work," Rafael said. "Good thinking, guys."

They found some branches. And they cut four poles. Then they carried them to the small river.

They moved the huge log into the water. It was heavy! They climbed on top. Then they pushed off with their poles. The log started to float across.

They were in the middle of the river. Then Lilia shouted, "Dad, *look*!"

Everyone turned. Their mouths dropped open. Their eyes got big.

Moving toward their log was a large snake. It was huge. They never saw a snake that large before! Its thick, green body was 20 feet long. And it looked hungry!

Rafael breathed hard. "Keep poling for the other shore!" he yelled.

The snake opened its huge mouth.

Rafael lifted his pole high. He brought it down on the snake's head. The huge snake was stunned.

Finally, they reached the far shore. Everyone climbed to safety.

They stopped to look back. They looked down at the water.

"I'm pretty sure that was an anaconda," Rafael said. "The largest snake in the world."

"I'm scared. I wish we were back home. Back in the Heights," Lilia said. She looked at her older brother. "Are you scared, Franco?"

"Who wouldn't be?" Franco said. "That monster was coming for us. I was scared to death! That was a huge snake!"

"We need to stay strong. We need to keep walking. No matter how scared we are," Rafael continued. "We'll be okay."

Chapter 8

Later in the day, Lilia stopped. She pointed up.

"What are those?" she asked.

"Those are palm trees. And those are coconuts!" Franco cried.

"They sure are!" Rafael said.

"They're high up. How do we get them down?" Antonio asked.

"Let's shake the tree. That's the easy way. Some should fall. We need to get the tree moving," said Rafael. "Come on, everyone. Let's get together. Now push!"

They pushed the tree. It hardly moved.

"Keep pushing!" Rafael said.

The tree started to move. It moved back and forth. Soon coconuts fell. The Silvas had to move. They didn't want to get hit.

Six coconuts fell. They peeled a coconut. Underneath was a hard, brown shell.

"Try to break a few coconuts. Use this rock," Rafael told the boys. "I'll work on making a hole. We can get the milk from inside."

An hour later, they were full. They ate coconut. And they drank the milk.

The Silvas moved through the jungle. It thinned out a bit. In some places, they could see far ahead.

They saw several wild pigs. The pigs ran out of the jungle. Everyone stared. The pigs jumped into the river!

Then the river began to bubble. Something was making it bubble. It was under the water! Suddenly, the wild pigs were dragged under. They disappeared. There was blood in the water. Lilia let out a scream. Now they could see hundreds of small fish. They were eating the pigs!

"Piranha!" Rafael cried. "They'll eat anything that moves."

The excited piranha were jumping.

They jumped out of the water. In less than two minutes there was nothing left of the pigs.

The family heard loud sounds. The sounds were above them. Monkeys and birds were also heading for the river.

Rafael looked worried.

Franco was the first to notice. There were ants. He pointed to several lines of ants. They were across their path.

"What's going on? There sure are a lot of ants here," he said.

"Quick!" Rafael yelled. "Get to the river. Go as fast as you can."

As the three kids followed their father, Antonio said, "Dad, why are we running from a few little ants?"

"Ants are dangerous. In the jungle they are deadly," Rafael said. "They travel in huge armies. And eat everything in their path."

They reached the river. The water was bubbling.

"It's the piranha!" Franco called out. "They're attacking everything. The water isn't safe!"

"What are we going to do?" Lilia cried out. "We're trapped! The piranha will get us in water. The ants will get us on land!"

Chapter 9

Antonio thought fast. "Why don't we climb a tree?" he said.

"The ants climb trees. But not one kind! There's one tree they can't climb," Rafael said. "It's called the ironwood. The wood is as tough as iron. Saws can't cut it. Axes bounce off of it. The ants can't climb it. We have to find that tree now. Spread out, guys. Look for a tree that has a dark, black trunk."

The number of ants doubled. The Silvas searched. They needed the ironwood tree.

Everywhere they walked, they had to step on ants. Soon the ants started to run up their legs. Their bites stung. Rafael finally found an ironwood tree.

There was a low branch. It was still high. Franco threw the rope over the branch.

Franco climbed up. He pulled Lilia up to safety. Antonio came next. Then Rafael got off the ground. His legs were covered with ants. He brushed them off. Too late! His legs were covered with bites.

They watched in wonder. Millions

of ants passed below them. The Silvas sat for hours. They watched the army of ants.

Finally, there were fewer ants. Rafael was sure there would be no more ants. He slid down the rope. One by one, the kids came after him.

Tired and hungry, the Silvas found a soft spot away from the river. Within a few minutes, they settled down. And they fell deeply asleep.

Chapter 10

By morning, the bites on Rafael's legs felt a little better.

"We might reach the village today. If we're lucky," he said.

At noon, Franco looked up the Amazon. He saw a wooden dock. It stuck out into the river.

"Dad!" he cried. "I can see a dock ahead. It looks like the village dock. I think we made it."

They had been here just days earlier. The Melo family lived here. They got off the boat at this dock.

But something was wrong. Where were the people?

"Nobody's here," Antonio said.

"Everyone must have left. They had to escape the ants," Rafael said. "But they'll be back. The ants are gone now. Guys, there's got to be a radio. Let's spread out. Look around until we find one."

Antonio found a radio. It took 10 minutes.

Rafael turned on the radio. He made a call. He called his job site.

He tried a few times. Then they heard a voice.

"Rafael, where are you? Are you

all right? Your kids all right? We've been searching!"

"We're fine. We're in a little village. It's downriver," Rafael said. "The whole place is deserted. I think they ran from the ants. We're okay. But we're hungry!"

"We'll send the chopper," the man on the radio said.

Rafael put down the radio. He sighed. He was relieved.

"It looks like the worst is over," he said. "A chopper will have us out of here. It will be here in a few hours."

Rafael and his family sat down on a bench. They waited.

The chopper was overhead. The pilot found a place to land.

"Glad everyone's all right, Rafael," the pilot said.

"We've had an adventure hiking through the jungle," Rafael said.

"I'll bet you have," the pilot replied. "I can't wait to hear all about it. Parts of the *Amazon Queen* were found. The boat went over the waterfall. We feared the worst."

Rafael said, "We all need a hot shower. And a good meal."

"Hop on board. I'll get you there," the pilot said. "And there's a surprise waiting for you! Mrs. Silva flew in yesterday. She's been worried sick."

The chopper flew fast. They arrived. When it was safe, Ana Silva ran to them. She hugged them. Tears streamed down her face.

Walking away from the chopper, Ana turned to Rafael. She said, "What's your next trip with the kids? Rafael sighed. He knew Ana wanted everyone safe. She wanted everyone back home in the Heights.